March
2019

For Yolanda—
I am so grateful to
know you, and more
conversations, please.
With ♡ and admiration.

[bon aire projects]

MAISON FEMME:
a fiction

Teresa Carmody *vanessa place*

INTRODUCTION
Danielle Pafunda / Reagan Louise

//
[bon aire projects]

//

ISBN-13: 978-0-9915820-1-3

Bon Aire Projects is supported in part by the generous funding of the Gray Chair (Steve McCaffery), the McNulty Chair (Dennis Tedlock), and the English Department at SUNY Buffalo.

//

Acknowledgments:
Textual, visual and introductory excerpts are forthcoming in *Faultline*.

Earlier versions of "Foyer" and "Front Porch" first appeared in *Two Serious Ladies* under the title "Two Rooms."

"Basement" appeared as "Basement" in *Entropy*.

Very early excerpts were incorporated in a panel presentation on publishing at the Queer Poetics Symposium, Naropa University, March 2014.

Thank you to Terry Castle for editing *The Literature of Lesbianism*, which thoroughly informs this book. Thank you to the many people who provided support, encouragement, and feedback on this project, including: Kanaka Agrawal, Mona Awad, Mildred Barya, Sarah Boyer, Melissa Buzzeo, Maired Byrne, Vincent Carafano, Serena Chopra, Lucy Corin, Emily Culiton, Lindsey Drager, Nick Gulig, Dana Green, Brandi Homan, Scott Howard, Laird Hunt, Haley Littleton, Emily Motzkus, Pam Ore, Bin Ramke, Christopher Rosales, Selah Saterstrom, Prageeta Sharma, Abigayil Wernsman, and Andrew Wessels.

Thanks especially to Amanda Ackerman and Harold Abramowitz.

Thank you to Danielle Pafunda and Reagan Louise, and to Amanda Montei and Jon Rutzmoser for making Bon Aire Projects.

And to Maude and Fergus Place: our hearts and always.

//

www.bonaireprojects.com

/ INTRODUCTION /

Danielle Pafunda
& Reagan Louise

Welcome to Maison Femme, mother foxers.

It's the crisis jubilee of property.
What's proper about property?
What props the property the proper proprietor.
What was property profits property.
A prop.
On the landing.
Propped.

The object is to make the play in three stories.

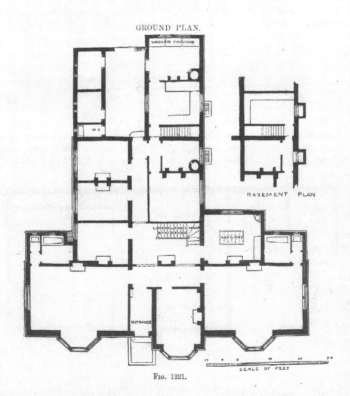

GROUND PLAN.

BASEMENT PLAN

SCALE OF FEET

Fig. 1221.

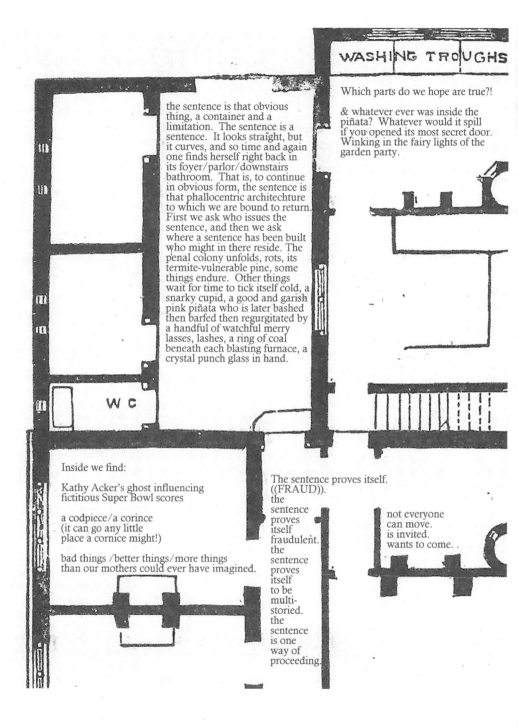

the sentence is that obvious thing, a container and a limitation. The sentence is a sentence. It looks straight, but it curves, and so time and again one finds herself right back in its foyer/parlor/downstairs bathroom. That is, to continue in obvious form, the sentence is that phallocentric architechture to which we are bound to return. First we ask who issues the sentence, and then we ask where a sentence has been built who might in there reside. The penal colony unfolds, rots, its termite-vulnerable pine, some things endure. Other things wait for time to tick itself cold, a snarky cupid, a good and garish pink piñata who is later bashed then barfed then regurgitated by a handful of watchful merry lasses, lashes, a ring of coal beneath each blasting furnace, a crystal punch glass in hand.

Which parts do we hope are true?!

& whatever ever was inside the piñata? Whatever would it spill if you opened its most secret door. Winking in the fairy lights of the garden party.

Inside we find:

Kathy Acker's ghost influencing fictitious Super Bowl scores

a codpiece/a corince
(it can go any little
place a cornice might!)

bad things /better things/more things
than our mothers could ever have imagined.

W C

The sentence proves itself.
((FRAUD)).
the
sentence
proves
itself
fraudulent.
the
sentence
proves
itself
to be
multi-
storied.
the
sentence
is one
way of
proceeding.

not everyone
can move.
is invited.
wants to come. .

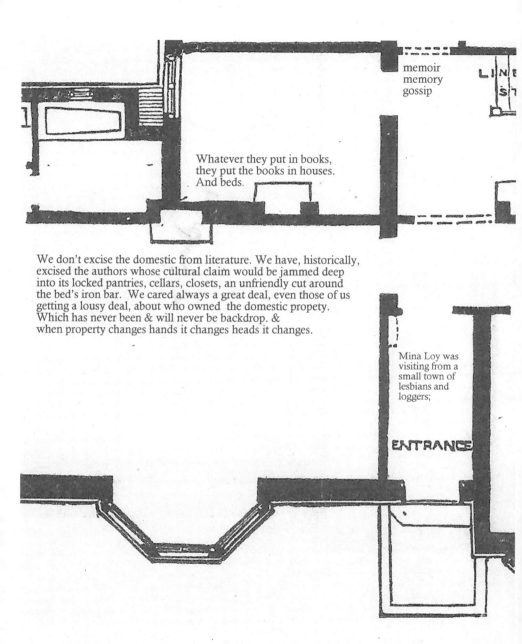

memoir
memory
gossip

LINE
ST

Whatever they put in books,
they put the books in houses.
And beds.

We don't excise the domestic from literature. We have, historically,
excised the authors whose cultural claim would be jammed deep
into its locked pantries, cellars, closets, an unfriendly cut around
the bed's iron bar. We cared always a great deal, even those of us
getting a lousy deal, about who owned the domestic propety.
Which has never been & will never be backdrop. &
when property changes hands it changes heads it changes.

Mina Loy was
visiting from a
small town of
lesbians and
loggers;

ENTRANCE

FIG

PLAN.

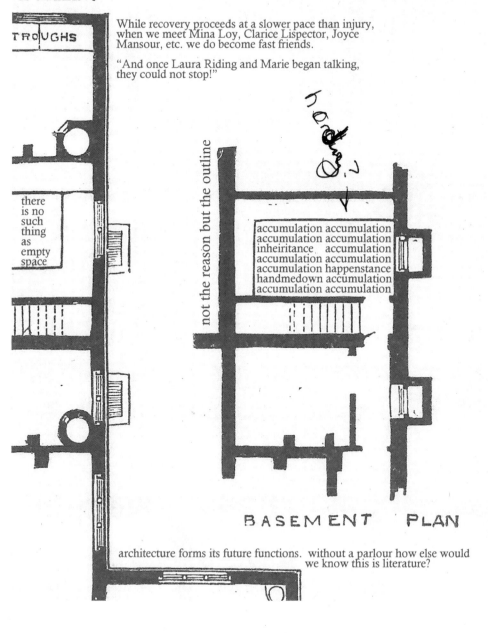

TROUGHS

While recovery proceeds at a slower pace than injury, when we meet Mina Loy, Clarice Lispector, Joyce Mansour, etc. we do become fast friends.

"And once Laura Riding and Marie began talking, they could not stop!"

there
is no
such
thing
as
empty
space

not the reason but the outline

accumulation accumulation
accumulation accumulation
inheiritance   accumulation
accumulation accumulation
accumulation happenstance
handmedown accumulation
accumulation accumulation

BASEMENT PLAN

architecture forms its future functions. without a parlour how else would
we know this is literature?

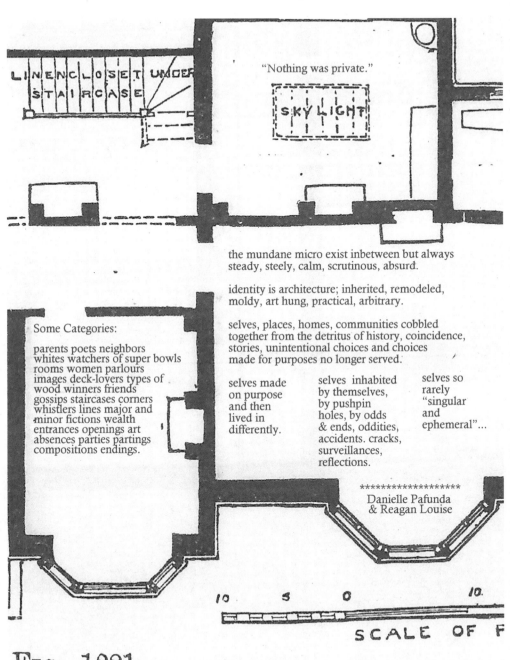

LINEN CLOSET UNDER
STAIRCASE

"Nothing was private."

SKYLIGHT

the mundane micro exist inbetween but always
steady, steely, calm, scrutinous, absurd.

identity is architecture; inherited, remodeled,
moldy, art hung, practical, arbitrary.

selves, places, homes, communities cobbled
together from the detritus of history, coincidence,
stories, unintentional choices and choices
made for purposes no longer served.

Some Categories:

parents poets neighbors
whites watchers of super bowls
rooms women parlours
images deck-lovers types of
wood winners friends
gossips staircases corners
whistlers lines major and
minor fictions wealth
entrances openings art
absences parties partings
compositions endings.

selves made
on purpose
and then
lived in
differently.

selves inhabited
by themselves,
by pushpin
holes, by odds
& ends, oddities,
accidents. cracks,
surveillances,
reflections.

selves so
rarely
"singular
and
ephemeral"...

****
Danielle Pafunda
& Reagan Louise

10   5   0   10.

SCALE OF F

FIG. 1221.

/ MAISON FEMME: A FICTION /

Teresa Carmody, text
Vanessa Place, images

for
Pam Ore

You can see it is difficult very difficult that history can ever come to be literature. But it would be so very interesting if it could be so very interesting.

-Gertrude Stein

Dear Reader,
This may not be about you,
but it's definitely about your friends.

INDEX OF IMAGES PROPERLY NAMED
(IN ORDER OF APPEARANCE)

CAST OF CHARACTERS PROPERLY NAMED
(IN ORDER OF APPEARANCE)

Marie	Andy Warhol
Louise	Dennis Cooper
Henry	Jean Rhys
Alisa Washington	Red
Jonathon Washington	Marianne Moore
Joelle Washington	Julia Kristeva
Mrs. Washington	Colette
Mina Loy	Miss Furr
Mr. & Mrs. Whittle	Miss Skeene
Robert	Leonora Carrington
Parker	James Tiptree, Jr.
Clarice Lispector	Phoebe Gloeckner
Gwen Harwood	Donald Barthelme
Laura Riding	Esther McCoy
Franz Kafka	Claire Denis
Leslie Scalapino	Vija Celmins

PANTRY

Marie looked out the pantry window. The neighbor had painted his house electric blue, stopping just below the attic window and leaving the top part unpainted. Mrs. Whittle said that's where the neighbor's ladder stopped, but Marie did not agree. The paint was chipped and unevenly faded; if Marie squinted her eyes, the house looked like a painting.

Marie was in the pantry because that's where they kept the garden party supplies, along with many other rarely used but periodically useful objects: an ice-cream maker, a bamboo mat, puzzles and board games, the children's box of art materials. Marie and Louise were hosting a garden party that day as a fundraiser, and Marie thought about inviting her neighbor. She would have liked to have her neighbor there, but then again, she did not want to charge her neighbor the door fee and her neighbor might not like the writers. He would not like their writing and he would not know anyone or have anyone to talk to. If her neighbor came to the party, Marie would feel like a good neighborly person, but doing something in order to see and be seen as a good person was a rather self-centered reason, and Marie did not want to be selfish. In the pantry, she found the punch bowl and several clear plastic serving trays.

Perhaps, thought Marie, she was being too quick a judge, for a person never could tell what she might herself like one day, and this sounded like Zola in *Nana*. Zola wanted to write every thing about every kind of person and life, so he described monstrous-enormous-swelling lesbians at a lesbian bar in Paris; Marie had heard that his book, published in 1880, was the very first scene of a lesbian bar in mainstream European literature. Marie liked poetry readings and literary events more than lesbian bars; she liked reading more than drinking though she would definitely drink a glass or more of spiked strawberry lemonade at the garden party, where there would be many lesbians of varying shapes and sizes, plus gay boys and other homos, married poets, unspecified straights, and, as part of a performance, women who would tie themselves to each other with thick ropes as they sang words from an anthology of women's writing. If Marie were to describe such a scene, should and could she try to include every kind of person present, how many details would make for a description as real and naturalistic as Zola, and when would details swell it into something gruesome, frightening, and obviously fake?

Marie liked to consider these kinds of questions, and she also liked to talk with her neighbor, who had served both in the Navy and in the Marines. He had worked, too, for the VA doing construction, and when it came to the VA, he had, quite understandably, very many complaints. On the front of

his electric blue house hung a Purple Heart flag, and sometimes he wore a Buffalo Soldier t-shirt; sometimes, he told
Marie about the fun-trouble he had while enlisted, and he
liked to say he was still following orders, but now the must-
dos came from his wife.

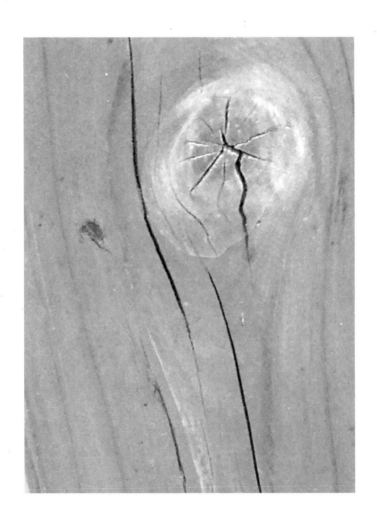

Louise?

BACK UPSTAIRS PORCH

The door to the back upstairs porch was unlocked again. "Oh dear," said Marie, "I better not tell Louise." She stepped outside and quickly closed the door behind her. Out there, nothing was private; Marie could see into the neighbors' yards, and the neighbors could see her standing awkwardly behind the porch's railing painted yellow-cream. The wood railing reached just past Marie's knees—she could easily trip over it!—but the back upstairs porch was the best spot for checking outside temperatures while surveying the grounds.

It was finally cooling down, thought Marie, as she looked at Henry's white camper, parked permanently in the Washington's backyard. Henry had shown up at the Washington's house when he was twenty-one years old and twenty years later, he still lived in the camper and often sat, as he was that evening, on the back deck with Alisa, Jonathon, and Joelle— the three of Mrs. Washington's adult children who lived at home with their mother and Uncle Cooper. The neighbors waved at Marie and Marie waved at the neighbors. They sat in big deck-style swivel chairs, playing the radio, drinking wine, and eating kettle chips—at least that's what it looked like to Marie. The one time Joelle had invited Marie and Louise over for drinks, they had declined, though during the holidays, Marie made a point to visit Mrs. Washington, swapping big slices of sweet potato or pumpkin pie.

Washington
↓
Alisa
Jonathon
Joelle
+
Henry

When Marie worked in the garden, she often heard Henry mumbling as he moved from one chore to another, and like the other adult children, he called Mrs. Washington *ma*. But Henry wasn't there the day Alisa came outside alone and whispered for Marie to come closer. "I used to have a girlfriend," said Alisa, "but my sister wouldn't have it." She looked at Marie very intensely to see if there was under-standing. "I had to move home to help take care of my ma, and my sister wouldn't have it; she said she wouldn't share a room with me, and if my ma found out, it would do her in."

Marie thought about this conversation later that day as she read Valentine Ackland's memoir, written as an apologia to Sylvia Townsend Warner because Valentine was planning on leaving Sylvia for an American woman with whom she was having an affair. But Valentine didn't leave; she stayed and as she aged, she returned to her family's Catholicism, and her swelling devotion was said to upset Sylvia more than any of her many affairs. After Valentine died, Sylvia published a collection of Valentine's poems, and even later, during a time when lesbians were learning their lesbian histories, Ackland's memoir was published with its original title: *For Sylvia: An Honest Account*. "My sister likes you and Louise," Alisa had said, "but she made me go meet my girlfriend—over by the park I met her and told her I couldn't meet her anymore." In

Valentine & Sylvia ≠ Amer. Woman
Catholic

her memoir, Valentine described the look on her father's face when he first learned about his daughter's lesbianism; his lip pulled up, his brows pressed closer, and his eyes went blank and beady with disgust as he surveyed the now unfamiliar body before him.

On the back upstairs porch, Marie watched Alisa laugh with Joelle, Jonathon, and Henry; the temperature had moved from cool to chilly, and Marie decided to look once more for the black corduroy jacket that had gone missing because it really truly did go best with her outfit, so it was the jacket she most wanted to wear.

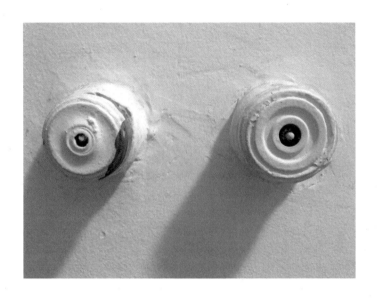

* The Mis-
understood
Vanessa
The Cry for
meaning
* The
Fear of
Abstraction

FRONT FOYER

"This is a photo of a dodo," said Marie. She pointed to a photograph of a dodo drawn in pencil, and Mina Loy looked. Above the photograph hung the dodo drawing, set in double glass and framed in wood. Mina Loy was visiting from a small town full of lesbians and loggers; the women stood together in the foyer and the walls were full of art. "The artist," said Marie, "likes to use a material that rhymes with what it is." "This is not strange," said Mina Loy, "rhyme is a very good reason." Marie and Mina Loy liked to discuss this question together: "What are people not supposed to do in life and writing?" "They are not supposed to write a book made of only one sentence," said Mina Loy. "If they are women," said Marie, "they are not supposed to violently disagree, at least not face-to-face."

"Art," said Marie, "used to feel like a very strange reason." Art was like racehorse breeds and fancy cheese. Marie had grown up in a small town in the middle of the country, a town surrounded by small farms and a general feeling that farmers' daughters aren't supposed to be artists, for except in some country music songs, farmers' daughters are wholesome and clean, and horses just pull things. Long ago, before Marie and Louise were Marie and Louise, Mina Loy told Marie to read Louise's sentence. "It is best to read it in one sitting," said Mina Loy, "and it is best to find a setting as uncomfortable

Marie & Louise = Teresa · B · Vanessa?

as the sentence." In the sentence, a legless soldier narrates his final night, for come the dawn he will die, and death is also a sentence for you and me. Long ago, Louise was in a weekly writing group, but when she gave the sentence to the other writers, they asked her to leave. "The sentence makes us angry," said one of the weekly writers. They liked to know exactly what meaning was happening, but the sentence fell and bled and held the phrase *crisis jubilee.*

"Word play is a very good reason," said Mina Loy, who was quite fond of Pierre de Bourdeilles's *donna con donna.* "Do you know," she told Marie, "there are lesbian weasels, which is why lesbians were represented by weasels in times before." "The dodo was extinct before the camera was invented, which is why the artist needed to draw a dodo to make her photo." A writing teacher told Louise she wrote too much like a man and this was a problem; another professor asked her if she was writing in drag. "I have known some lesbians who are very much like men," said Marie, but when she later considered this statement, she did not know what it could mean. In the foyer, Mina Loy placed her keys on Louise's grandmother's writing desk, which was kidney shaped and made of tulip wood. "We know someone who asked her students to punctuate the sentence," said Marie, "and there was such disagreement about which clauses belonged together, it proved the sentence's grammatical truth."

"Dodos and weasels and lesbians and loggers," sighed Mina Loy. "What would you like to drink?"

BEDROOM 1

Mr. Whittle had sat in the southwest bedroom while he worked on his writing. His handshake was firm and when he shook Marie's hand, he placed his left hand on top of her right hand and looked her in the eye. He was being sincere and authentic so that Marie would know his genuine presence. The Whittles had sold the house to Louise and Marie and moved to a wealthy neighborhood near the ocean. Mrs. Whittle worked in finance in an office on the Westside, and the children attended expensive private schools. Living in the wealthy neighborhood would make the commute much calmer. Before a great many people in the neighborhood began losing their houses, there was a set designer who lived in the green house two doors down from Louise and Marie. She told Marie that Mr. Whittle had worked on a television show popular in the 1980s; it was a show about white people making their professional ways while having problems with their best friends and others. When the Whittles bought the house, the show was still on television. Inside their new house, the Whittles stripped the paint covering the wood-work, and outside, they put up a white picket fence.

The Whittles did not speak to Marie about spirits in the house. Instead, they said the neighbors were friendly—the friendliest neighborhood ever—and on the day they decided to move, Mrs. Whittle began to cry. She cried for three days as she dug in the dirt and weeded her garden of daylilies and lilac and yarrow. Mr. Whittle stayed in the southwest bedroom, redone as his office, and he sat and typed and he did not hear Mrs. Whittle or any other strange noises. When Mrs. Whittle was upset, she played the piano very loudly; in the yard, she planted and planted and made everything green. When spoons and tools disappeared from their set places, the Whittles often blamed each other, and only sometimes were these things found later, clearly misplaced. Sometimes the door to Mr. Whittle's office was open, though Mr. Whittle was sure he had closed it. When he was younger, Mr. Whittle was known as quite the Casanova, at least that is what he believed as he taught fitness classes at the YMCA. He taught classes because the writing was going slower and slower, but Mr. Whittle believed in certain things, like looking another person in the eye. Marie heard stories about the Whittles while talking to the neighbors, and sometimes when she was gathering lemons or limes or blood oranges from the backyard trees, she remembered Mrs. Whittle saying how important the fruit trees were to their son. When Marie bought a new porch mat with a special design and certain house-matching colors, she thought the purchase very Whittle-like of her.

Was it Whittle-like of Giacomo Casanova, thought Marie, to write lesbian scenes of which he was the center?

His scenes always included at least two females plus himself, and he called his book a memoir and titled it *A History of My Life*, and such a title does look a reader right in the eye. Yet Marie wondered: are the women in Casanova's scenes lesbians or lesbian-like, and how long must a person live in a neighborhood before becoming a full-on neighbor? When the Whittles told Marie about the day they decided to move, they spoke of their inevitable sadness because the time they knew would always come had finally arrived. Marie and Louise, on the other hand, had not foreseen their finding a big house on a neighborly street in a major metropolis, and they found the house quite by accident, or more specifically, Louise was online, researching a house in another neighborhood when her finger slipped, leading them to this one, with its giant honey-pot basement large enough for several desks and half a dozen pallets of books.

FRONT PORCH

Louise handed the pink pony to Marie and asked if she liked it. Marie liked it; it was a fine piñata, with a dark pink mane and plain black eyes. Louise had picked out the pony at a nearby market with the help of their son. "We almost bought a turtle," he later told Marie as they hung the piñata from a hook on the front porch, thus marking their house apart from the others. "A turtle would have been nice," said Marie, "very protective." "But ponies are better for parties," said their son, and Marie agreed that the pony was just right.

At the house that evening, Marie and Louise were hosting a benefit auction to raise money needed to make books of other people's writing. The evening was filled with items both singular and ephemeral; there was, for example, a cake baked by a public high school English teacher who was an excellent baker and also the alumnus of a famously exclusive private university. There were prints and photographs by artists with big and small reputations; several poets, all of them female, donated several kinds of services, including commissioned poems, palm readings, and tarot consultations.

The cake was round, butterscotch, and made with many layers. It was purchased by a poet who had donated a commissioned poem, a poet known across the country for both her poetry and her lesbianism. Three years later, the poet would, in fact, publish a novel about becoming a lesbian and becoming a poet, a novel based on many true stories from the poet's young life in New York.

Later, Marie would read this novel during a one week stay at a cheap hotel in the desert. Marie was in the desert to work on her own novel, which was neither about lesbianism nor poetry, and as Marie read the poet's novel, she noted its fine sentences and saw that the book contained both a character and a dog named Marie. Earlier, Marie had written two sentences by Jane Bowles on a small piece of paper: "'I love my country,' said Sis, for no apparent reason. 'I love it to death.'" Marie used this piece of paper as a bookmark in the poet's novel.

Marie had brought her large dog to the hotel in the desert, and every morning they walked together on a baseball field she had discovered on the hill behind the hotel. Other women with dogs also walked on this field every morning, and these women, who lived in the small desert town and who were partially retired but still held part-time positions as sales clerks and dental receptionists, took Marie into their group because she was, in some ways, like them. Marie's big dog liked to play with their big dogs, and Marie talked with the women about their dogs and holiday cooking, for it was early December and one woman made cheese balls every year at this time.

But on the last day of Marie's week-long stay, one of the women complained about Asians, though she used the word Oriental, and Marie looked directly at the woman and said that was not her experience. Marie spoke with the polite lightness of wanting to keep things pleasant. The woman who made cheese balls quickly changed the subject, and less than a few minutes later, Marie said it was time for her to go. All week the women had spoken to Marie as if Marie had a husband, and Marie did not correct them, but used a tone of camaraderie as she spoke about parenting. Everyone knows most parents are not lesbians, and pink piñatas are rather gay, so a few months after the first benefit auction, Marie and Louise filled the pony with candy and presented it as a birthday gift to the poet who had written about her young lesbian life.

A complimentary image of the lesbian poet smashing the pink piñata later surfaced in a manifesto by a new narrative writer, and the lesbian poet is still friends with this writer, but she did not stay friendly with Louise and Marie for lesbianism alone was not enough to keep bringing them together, and the lesbian poet had decided Louise did not support her work.

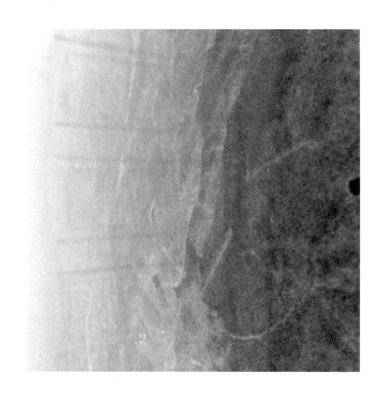

Second Parlor

Louise began calling the second parlor The Parlor and the front parlor The Front Parlor, and as Marie had always wanted a parlor, she agreed. Having two parlors turned their house into literature, because in Marie's experience, the only people with parlors were people in books. Her neighbor with the electric blue house, for example, did not have a parlor, though he did have a den, as that was what he called his front room and he furnished it with three dark leather couches and a very large television.

Marie sank into one of these couches one Sunday to watch the Super Bowl with her neighbor, his wife, and several of his friends; Marie did not care about football, but her neighbor had made it a point to invite her and Louise. "I told the others I invited you," he told Marie one day as they stood together on the front sidewalk beneath a large sweetgum tree. Marie nodded, and he said something else, too, about right and wrong and what makes good people, and Marie understood then there had been conversations about how lesbians were living in the neighborhood and this was new. Marie and Louise were not, however, the first white people in the neighborhood; the Whittles were white as were the young straight couple who lived on the other side of Mrs. Washington's house. There was also the divorced community college math teacher whose only child, a son, received a full scholarship to law school; and finally, there was Henry with his camper parked in Mrs. Washington's backyard.

At the Super Bowl party, Marie talked to Robert, who lived across the street and was the single dad of a grown son and two children still in elementary school. Marie did not know the story of the children's mother and did not ask, as she would not welcome similar questions about the father of her and Louise's children. At the Super Bowl party, Robert's younger children sat on wooden chairs placed close together near the den doorway, and they ate thick slices of lemon cake as their eyes moved back and forth between the game on television and the couches filled with adults eating chicken wings and beans and tiny weenies. Robert asked Marie who she was betting on, but Marie didn't know who was playing, so said she was undecided and this technically was true. She asked Robert who was performing the half-time show, and several people chimed in—"Madonna!"—and her neighbor teased her for always working and not paying attention to anything else, as his friends looked on with slight suspicion, for how could she not know!

Later, Madonna was surrounded by men dressed as Roman gladiators, and Marie considered the currency of cultural information and how so many so-called classic books include parlor scenes because so many of these books were written by and about the upper-class. At the Super Bowl party, everyone agreed Madonna was slightly unsteady and the commercials were also a spectacle of American capitalism, selling stuff for distraction, and in this way, at least to Marie, the commercials were not unlike the game. After the half-time show, she sunk even further into the couch, a second serving of beans on her paper plate as she watched the men in tight pants roll around with each other, and they reminded her of Anthony Hamilton's *Memoirs of the Life of Count Grammont*, published in 1713. Hamilton's book was filled with gossip about the court of Charles II, and Marie was very interested in the small battle between Lord Rochester and Miss Hobart over the affections of the young and talented Miss Temple. Lord Rochester tried to woo Miss Temple with his compositions, saying he did not think it proper to flatter a young woman by speaking of her accomplishments, so he spoke, instead, about his other favorite subject, which happened to be himself. Miss Hobart warned Miss Temple away from Lord Rochester, a man who habitually wooed young women but never asked for their hand; Miss Hobart lied, however, when she said Lord Rochester was speaking ill of Miss Temple, and this lie came to haunt her. For in the end, and according to Anthony Hamilton, a dramatic boudoir scene played out between the two Misses, in which Miss Temple saw Miss Hobart as an eager satyr, or, if possible, "some monster still more odious," and disengaging "herself with the highest indignation from [Miss Hobart's] arms, [Miss Temple] began to shriek and cry in the most terrible manner, calling both heaven and earth to her assistance." And so, as the story goes, Lord Rochester won.

Marie had read the story of Miss Hobart, Miss Temple, and Lord Rochester while sitting on the big green chair in the second parlor, which is where Marie and Louise also kept their copy of *The Literature of Lesbianism*, edited by a writer and scholar who is known to love women in books and in bed. When Marie looked up, she could see a large color photograph that hung on the opposite wall. It framed a person's torso—white and likely female—from her shoulders to just above the knees; the person, dressed in black, held a black and white photograph against a red binder's diagonal pattern of solid white hearts inside outlines of larger white hearts. In the black and white photograph, four young white people stood around the blank space of a fifth person whose image had been cut out, leaving the outline of a body only. Behind the four figures hung an American flag; inside the outline of the missing person were the words: LIVE LIKE HIM.

Because Marie knew the artist who made the color photograph, she knew the photograph was from 2008, and that the black and white photograph inside the color photograph was from 1969. The missing figure was a member of the Weather Underground; he was staying with one of the men pictured in the black and white photograph because he needed a secret place to be. Marie knew this story from a video by the artist, also titled LIVE LIKE HIM; the video is a long take, up and down the stairs of the New York State capital building, as the viewer listens to a man—the man who hid the Weatherman—tell a story from that year, the drugs and truth-telling and near psychotic break, the fag-baiting and brokenness, and his conversations with Mike, the Weatherman, about sexism and homophobia and variant kinds of love.

Oh my, thought Marie, with a start, as one of the football teams scored a goal and the Super Bowl partiers let out a shout. Both teams, she noticed, had the same team colors—red, white and blue—and this seemed telling and as monstrously American as her own pick-and-choose thoughts, from Miss Temple and the court of Charles II, to lesbian scholars and the Weathermen and still, the neighbor who lived in the blue house remained unnamed. "Well, then," said Marie, later and to no one in particular, "his name will be Parker, because the letter *k* comes after *l*, and *e*, like *o*, is a vowel." Besides, Parker was known in the neighborhood for his orange traffic cone, which he frequently placed on the street as if it held official

capacity, and this was how he managed to save a spot, sometimes for himself and other times for Robert, who worked a
late-night shift, and who would know, in the very least, there
would be street parking at home.

DOWNSTAIRS HALLWAY

Louise wanted to rearrange the art in the downstairs hallway
to make it more visible. "If you don't see something," asked
Marie, "has it gone missing?" ?Susan
    "The problem," continued Marie, "is that it's not a hall-
way but a square space between four doors." Marie held a
small frame in a certain spot so Louise could see it. Louise
agreed, calling the space a crossroads and gesturing that
the piece was still too low; Marie moved the picture up two
inches. Inside the frame, a thick line of sea salt ran across
a white canvas, otherwise unmarked. The salt came from
a site-specific installation in which an artist gathered 180
gallons of seawater from the Santa Monica Bay and put the
water into a specially-made concrete pond inside a museum.
The pond was then covered with solar-powered lights and
fans, so the seawater evaporated leaving small piles of large
bone-colored crystals.
    "The puzzle of history," said Marie, "is the hiss of it, and
the way a snake carries both medicine and poison." Louise
conceded, though she defended *Mrs. Dalloway* as Virginia
Woolf's best book. "Yet all of the lesbians in *Mrs. Dalloway*
quit being lesbians," said Marie, "the older Sally Seaton clings
to her five boys and Miss Kilman—by the way, Mina Loy
thinks Woolf modeled Miss Kilman on Natalie Barney, and
Mina calls Woolf a coward and says she wrote lesbians as

the process = the result

Spoken word
  's
Literary? | poetry

My influences

monstrous and barefooted as any found in the history of English literature—Miss Kilman clings to the church." Louise said she understood but disagreed and suggested moving the small green 'I do math' picture into the hallway. It was bright enough to be noticed and the words would caption the space.

We write us → ? the extended us =
niegbors
Enemies
family
Earth
other animals

DECK

Marie and Louise would not have a grill if the Whittles had not left their large grill behind. The grill was on the back deck, and for many years, the back deck railings were covered with trumpet flower vines which bloomed, it seemed, year round. The vines swelled the railings to twice their size, and also ran beneath the deck floor, creating a dark wet spidery space between the plant and the wood. Beneath the deck there was also a not-so-secret door to the basement, and in the summer, this was the most used door of the house.

In general, Marie and Louise were not deck-loving lesbians, though it is difficult to not admire a well-built deck. The Whittles had built this particular deck, or rather, the Whittles hired men to plan and build the deck, and the Whittles ordered pine instead of cedar or redwood or cypress and this was their first mistake for pine is not termite-repellent. The Whittles also placed large flower pots directly on the deck's surface, which created, along with the vine, an ideal atmosphere for rot. Marie hired men to move the flower pots off the deck and to replace the rotting floor, but Marie cut the trumpet vine herself one evening; as she worked, she listened to a lecture on mostly forgotten Old English poetry, cutting and pulling until it was quite dark and creating a pile of dying and dead vine bigger and wider than Marie.

"What does it mean to be on deck?" said Marie. She was speaking to Clarice Lispector, who was visiting from Brooklyn. Clarice Lispector was a poet, a clairvoyant, and also a lesbian, though like Marie, she rarely went to dyke marches or picnics for she had very few non-writer, non-artist friends. "There is no difference between life and writing," said Clarice Lispector. "This was what we continued to remember: Book to story, story to book." Marie loved the way Clarice spoke in and outside image, and this also described Clarice's writing.

Marie had, in fact, become friends with Clarice Lispector through the process of publishing her poetry. Neither Marie nor Louise knew Clarice when they accepted her manuscript, and when Louise finally met Clarice in person, she phoned Marie and told her that she, too, must meet Clarice Lispector for she could easily imagine the two of them becoming quite good friends. Louise made this telephone call from a smallish city in the middle of the country where Louise, along with several other writers, was teaching in a summer writing program known for its experiments in poetry and open-mindedness. Marie and Louise also spoke about how so many believe there is one very particular way be open-minded, and that to rewrite embodiment through layers of trauma, an experiment in perception is as necessary as alcohol to a dirty wound.

In the world of poetry, there is rarely a clear line between a poet and a publisher, because most poetry is published by poets or writers who begin small presses. Yet Marie became friends with Clarice Lispector truly, and Clarice never considered Marie to be a wife and Louise a husband, nor Louise the wife and Marie the husband, and she also believed that poets and small press publishers were equally important, just like everyone has so much light inside them covered over with so much culture and trauma and so much more. Clarice agreed that perceptual experiments can shift the hierarchies inside us, and Marie said that being on deck was inevitable; perhaps the better question was: Do you know what deck you're on?

Through reading, Marie learned about Henry Fielding's pot-boiling pamphlet known as *The Female Husband*. The pamphlet is thought to be based on the true-life story of Mary Hamilton, a young cross-dresser who married a young woman named Mary Price. For three months of marriage, Mary Price did not know her husband's female body, and when she discovered this surprising news, she helped prosecute Mary Hamilton as a vagrant, for their rental lease was under *his* name, not *hers*, and Mary Hamilton, as

Mary Hamilton, did not have a home. Questions of insides and underneaths pressed on both Marie and Clarice Lispector. Over the years, Clarice helped many poets read their insides through her practice as a palm-reader; she also read Marie's palm, and this was how Marie began to re-image the word *fraud*.

In terms of publishing a friend's book of poetry: the process of publishing is filled with many pot holes and publishing is a business and business relationships are never about something as pure as poetry, though poetry, as we know, is not pure. Marie did not believe poets to be necessarily good people, which is to say, a generally better sort of person, though many poets, perhaps understandably, feel a great need to protect poetry and so they begin to consider poets as necessarily good.

Louise and Marie published many books of poetry by many women who did, in fact, copy words written in other places, and some said the books they published were not real poems. Nonetheless, the women published a book in which a female poet wrote: "Dora had, even at the age of eight, begun to develop neurotic symptoms like two breasts that are like two young roes that are twins, which feed among the lilies, and she would leak prenatal colostrums, express milk voluntarily with the aid of organic external pressure, express milk with the aid of inorganic external pressure, and express milk involuntarily when hearing me cry." In another book they published, another poet wrote: "She has / A Vulva / Labia Majora / And / A feminine / Urethra / Independent / Of / A sort of / Imperforate / Penis / Which / Might be / A / Monstrously / Developed / Clitoris." In still another book published by Louise and Marie, still yet another poet wrote: "The woods decay, the woods decay and fall, tongues where I've started to move between thy ground, a man who comes whilst tilling thy field. I lie with thee and handle thy clit, my swan, my cruel immortality." And in the beginning of her new book, Louise wrote: "Of shapes transformed to bodies strange, we propose to celebrate; / of eternal lines grown mute towards time, / we ungodded *emulate*." On a panel discussion about women and publishing, another female poet said women's writing is almost always critiqued as lesser and redundant, which is, thought Marie, another way to name a fraud.

"Did you know," said Marie, "some poets are thought to be 'not poet-friendly'?" Marie was speaking to Clarice Lispector and Gwen Harwood, another friend and a poet who had come to the house for a visit because Clarice was in town. "I learned this news," said Marie, "from a male poet who says Louise is not a real poet because some of her work is prose and he does not like her un-poetry." "But Marie," said Gwen with a sloppy nod, "that poet is seriously afraid of spiders..." and her voice trailed off for she was rather drunk. A deck is, after all, a place for having parties, and a party can be a space for losing focus, so the women sat together on the deck and it was evening and they were drinking red wine from small cheap glasses and Louise was in Oslo or Berlin or Paris or Copenhagen or some other place in some other country where she had been invited to present her poems to be unliked.

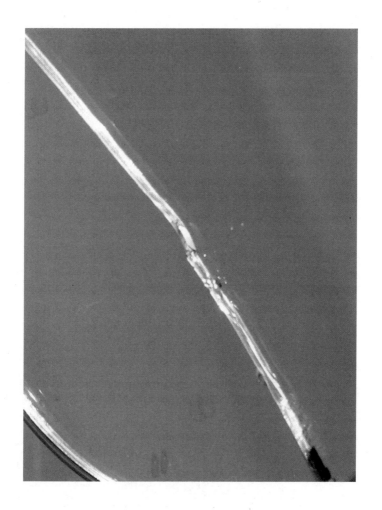

BACK STAIRCASE

"If you girls won't give me away, I'll show you something," wrote Mabel Dodge, using quotations to mark these words as Auntie Em's, the wonderfully strange aunt of Mable Dodge's childhood neighbor friends: Dorothy and Madeleine. The girls promised their secrecy, so Auntie Em left the room, reemerging minutes later dressed in a man's set of evening clothes. "'But you must remember now. You're not going to tell about these clothes. Your mother and father would burn them if they knew I had them in the house, girls,' she said, turning to Madeleine and Dorothy."

The winding back staircase at Marie and Louise's house was also unexpected; it was a narrow staircase behind a handleless door, and walking up it, Marie always found herself looking at another, smaller and also handleless door built into the staircase wall. The small door was jammed shut and would not open. Above it hung a Mission-style window with selected panes of colored glass; the window looked out onto nothing—there was a board behind it—but inside the window, in the pattern of colored panes, Marie could see what she thought of as abstract images of pussy-cat heads.

Sometimes when Marie sat in the second parlor, she could hear a dog run down the back staircase, though a dog never appeared. She only heard the dog in the early morning, so Marie liked to ask overnight guests who slept on the green couch in the second parlor if they had slept well and through the night. "I slept better here than I did at Mabel Dodge's house in Taos," said Gwen Harwood; she had recently taken a road trip through Arizona and New Mexico and had stayed at the Mabel Dodge Luhan House, now operating as a historic inn. "In Mabel Dodge's old library," continued Gwen, "is a low wooden door with a peacock engraved on it. Mabel's husband, Tony, carved it, though he had never seen a peacock; he followed Mabel's description only, and the wood is ponderosa pine."

"What is the purpose of your back staircase?" said Gwen Harwood with a sudden expression of surprise. Marie glanced in the direction of the handleless door and said she did not know, but she liked to imagine the older white lady who broke the racial covenant on the house's title as a progressively-minded heir of the original inhabitants. "She sold the house to an African American family," explained Marie, "because the father worked for the LAPD... I learned this from one of his children, who stopped by the house the other day because she wanted to see her childhood home, and she said they were the first black family on the block and it pissed the neighbors off because like many white people, the neighbors were mostly concerned with property values, and didn't want their investments burned up because black people were moving in. But instead of suing the former owner for violating the title's covenant, it sounds like the white people began moving out of the neighborhood instead."

BASEMENT

Louise and Marie drove away from the house, having rented it for the day to a production company that was filming a television commercial for an iconic brand of American beer. The beer commercial, entitled "Basement," would air later that year during football season. It featured a fan whose favorite team scored points every time he went into the scary basement to grab another beer. In the commercial, the basement was called "down there."

Marie and Louise called the basement The Press, or sometimes, The Basement, and when Marie was a child, "down there" referred to a body part her mother refused to name. The basement was only partially beneath ground—it had windows all around—and when Marie and Louise first saw it, they knew it was a place for making books. Louise liked to say the basement was the sole reason they bought this particular house, and some believed her. Before moving in, Marie hired a man to scrape and repair the basement's brick walls, and another man installed six electrical outlets, the exact placement of which Marie decided with some arbitrariness. The basement, after all, was the foundation of the house, and while it had been used for many other purposes—dancing and painting and storing things and games of hide and seek—it came with only one outlet and Marie could see stains on the floor where water sat during times of heavy rain.

Metaphors must matter, thought Marie as she looked at the giant L-strap anchors punctuating the basement walls, part of a retrofit after the Northridge earthquake. The women eventually put gutters on the house and this solved the flooding, so Marie could lie very easily on the large, maroon rug in the center of the basement, where she read Kathy Acker's sentences, which could be, thought Marie, about The Basement or The Press: "One cunt's like every other cunt. One ideal's like every other ideal. When one dream goes, another takes its place. You're sick of standing in this shit and so you step out."

Marie discovered that making a book recreated the book's insides; when she designed a book whose poems could be read forward, backward, or in a mirror, the publication process moved in this same way, and when she edited a book in which the narrative repeatedly undid itself, she saw her work repeatedly undone and the need for careful listening. One night, Marie sat shaking on a cheap office chair as she taped box after box and felt how thousands of books could drown her, and then she remembered her friend, Franz Kafka, telling her that very few people managed to be both a publisher and a writer. Another time, she traveled to New York for an artist residency, where she finished a draft of her novel, met Laura Riding, and once Laura Riding and Marie began talking, they could not stop! Laura Riding could read a book a day and a person in a minute, and the two women tended to drink too much together, and not because they planned on getting drunk, but because they talked so intently that one drink led to just a bit more. In the morning, they laughed at their naughtiness, and apologized (they were both habitual apologizers), even as they knew such an evening would happily happen again.

But long before her friendship with Laura Riding, Marie asked a number of other friends if they would please come over and help paint the basement. For this was the beginning of the basement becoming The Press, and The Press was, after all, a nonprofit organization, which means it was, technically and from the beginning, publically owned. (Marie paused to consider the +/- of nonprofit vs. for-profit, especially in the realm of publishing poetry, a topic on which she was becoming somewhat of an expert, which really meant knowing how much she did not know and could not do. In any case, Marie had sat on many panels about publishing, and while some asked how to start their own press, most of the time, on most of the panels, the audience wanted to know if Marie would publish them, and Marie wished they would buy books already published. This was a boring exchange, and Marie wondered how to make a different conversation, so she began fictionalizing her talks about publishing, telling listeners that when it came down to it, she and Louise were only interested in losers. "Failure is so popular these days," she said, "in poetry, failure is inevitable and good, but what are you willing to lose?" Other times she asked: "What is the writer in your head?") That day, the day of the painting, several friends gathered and painted, and this, in Marie's opinion, was how writing happened: people working together in conversation, one action, one thought, building one upon another, standing, as one poet wrote, on the shoulders of giants. Except we're not building what he wanted, thought Marie, and sometimes we're unbuilding. Because when that poet wrote "giant," he meant "genius," but Marie knew that most giants were short, unnamed volunteers with breasts and/or vaginas and/or scar tissue and/or kinky hair.

*

"The most beautiful room I ever saw," said Gwen Harwood as she wiped her mouth with a napkin, "had a cement floor colored with pigment." Gwen Harwood had helped with the basement painting, and after the friends were done for the day, they sat on the grass in the backyard eating greens, fried chicken, and peach cobbler. "You could buy pure pigment at the art supply store," continued Gwen, "and mix it into your cement coating material." "What is pure pigment?" asked Marie. Gwen Harwood, who used to be a painter, said artists used pigment to make their own paints. Later, Louise and Marie followed Gwen's advice and this is how the basement floor became dark cobalt blue.

"You know what else you need?" Dennis Cooper paused and waited for Marie to look at him. "Kathy Acker's desk." Marie gave a puzzled look just as Dennis Cooper looked away. "I have it back," he continued, and his gaze landed on a bit of cobbler which sat, quite unexpectedly, on Gwen Harwood's shoulder. "Kathy would like it to be there, do you know what I mean? As part of a feminist press." Dennis Cooper had been good friends with Kathy Acker; he was also the executor of her literary trust, and had, since her death, been taking care of her things. This was how the women came to not only have Kathy's desk, but her carpet, her dining room table, her side tables, her coffee table, and her big red reading chair. Evidently, Kathy was fond of the color red and also of velvet and leather, and because Kathy had not been a direct or early influence on either Marie or Louise's writing, Marie felt that they had not chosen Kathy as much as Kathy chose them. Kathy Acker continued to creep in: they bought a painting made in response to a German translation of *Blood and Guts in High School.* The artist lived in what had been East Berlin; the book was smuggled copy and the painting was abstract, which was, technically and at the time of its making, against the law. The women also published a book featuring a fictional Kathy Acker, and another book filled with random facts about Kathy, written by Dennis Cooper.

*

"What kinds of stories?" said Marie. It was later and the women were upstairs whispering in one of the bedrooms, their voices periodically interrupted by a couch full of actors cheering for a fictional football goal scored in a repeatedly filmed scene. Louise wanted to know the best stories from the basement, and Marie thought about the various poets who had slept on the single bed tucked in its northeast corner. There was not, she realized, a single interesting story to tell about the sleeping poets, and not because they weren't, to Marie and likely to others, interesting people who wrote and said many interesting things. But it is creepy to mine guests for stories and other bits of trade-gossip, and Marie had learned to be careful—some poets are weird! They say weird things about others, and share news that simply is not true! Yet she also believed gossip showed a healthy interest in the lives of others and that it would be good for some poets to think about someone else for awhile, but not in an envious or bitter way. It can be good, thought Marie, to imagine the subjectivity of another, as imagination makes us real.

"I have done many boring things in the basement," said Marie. "I have made countless budgets and written several introductions." Marie paused: "An introduction is not unlike the basement of a book." Louise looked skeptical. "It's the foundation," Marie continued, "or the parameters. Not the reason, but the outline."

"What," she asked, "is a basement filled with books published by lesbians?"

A few days prior, Marie had read the introduction to a big book previously mentioned, a book tracing representations of lesbianism in Western literature. It was, she learned, the recovery of Sappho in the 16th century that set a string of images in motion. It was, she learned, publishing that began to create a languaged illustration of this two-women-lesbian-thing. The book did not, however, answer her other questions. For example, one day Marie heard that people she did not know considered her and Louise to be man-hating lesbians. What a strange thing for them to be thinking! Then again, thought Marie, so many people are sadly stereotypical, and she wondered why strangers cared about her feelings for men. More importantly, thought Marie, why are there so few basements in Southern California?

Yet the truth was when Marie thought about the basement, she thought about Leslie Scalapino and Andy Warhol, an unlikely yet undeniably cute couple, and the evening they sat together stuffing envelopes with invitations. Leslie Scalapino was an intern then, and she was coordinating The Press's annual benefit auction, themed "As If." Marie and Leslie had invited others to please come over and join them, but only Andy came, meaning it was just the three of them and Marie had ordered Chinese food, so they could really have some fun. Before then, Marie hadn't spent much time with Andy Warhol, and Leslie later told Marie that he called her funny. This pleased Marie, for as the children could verify, funny was not a word people generally used to describe her. Later, after Leslie Scalapino married Andy Warhol, they asked Marie if she and Louise would make a book together, and Marie remembered the laughing and said yes.

I will write about the house, thought Marie, and how Louise said the basement was big enough for publishing. Marie licked her lips and imagined what they could do with the space.

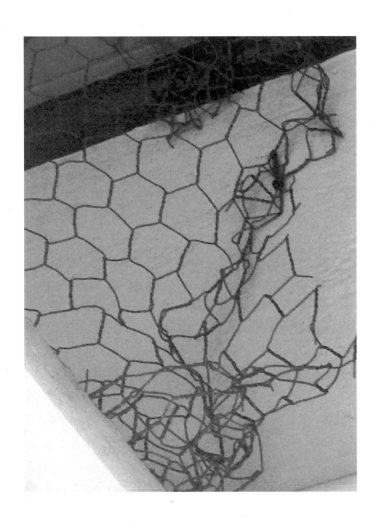

Basement Stairs

Marie slipped as she ran down the basement stairway, scraping her right buttock and the back of her thigh along several of the plain wooden steps. The pain was intense, so she sat on the bottom step for several minutes, staring at the basement's cinderblock wall, sucking in her breath, and saying *fuck fuck*. And *fuck* because there wasn't much time to prepare for the party at the distinguished scholar's house, held in honor of a talented poet from London. The talented poet, also a lesbian, was in Los Angeles to complete a special collaborative project at one of the art museums. Marie's buttocks and thighs were already turning dark purple, blue, black and red, but at the party, they were safely concealed beneath her houndstooth skirt. When she bought the skirt, she did not know the pattern's name, or even that it had one, for Marie did not come from a fashionable family, but from, as she liked to say, a long line of peasants. "My mom worked at the post office," Marie would say to certain people, "my dad built buildings, and neither of them went to college." As Marie became more knowledgeable of the world outside her childhood, she learned that such a history would sometimes earn her points, other times, scorn, and that among many educated people, being polite often demanded an assumed agreement of being from, or at least for, the middle class.

At the party, Louise spoke to the distinguished scholar, the talented poet, a recently tenured English professor and her novelist girlfriend, the two of whom, in a back-and-forth exchange with many interruptions, told Louise about the late 18th century poet Anna Stewart and her likely lesbianism. The story amused Louise almost as much as the women's style of telling. Across the room, Marie met some of the distinguished scholar's current students, including one who called herself Jean Rhys. Due, perhaps, to her second glass of wine, Marie forgot about her painful buttocks while she asked Jean Rhys about her research on the poetics of dislocation, and because Marie did not have a third glass of wine, she did not mention her parent's discomfort with anyone, including their children, who held post-secondary degrees. Later, Marie learned that Jean Rhys was sometimes a lesbian, and that the talented poet from London considered her own mother unbearably bourgeois.

Some time before or after the party (Marie can't remember), she learned about various writers' mothers at a consciousness raising event she helped to organize as part of a conference on feminism and experimental women's writing. The event was called "Eat Your Mother," and most of the mature (i.e., older) writers spoke easily about their mothers, laughing at the old criticisms and criticizing in turn, while many of the younger writers (i.e., including Marie) could only speak of their mothers as abstractions, for they were still inexperienced enough to feel their mothers raw.

FRONT WALKWAY

"A white picket fence," said the bearded poet with delight. He was speaking to Marie about the house and his voice was pleasant and sarcastic. He was making a comment, Marie noticed, but she did not know this poet enough to legibly read his words. They had been together for less than an hour, talking about his travels, his recent move, his new tenure-track job at the university. They had stopped at Marie and Louise's house to gather supplies for the evening, and as they moved through the rooms, Marie felt herself increasingly absent. The bearded poet, she realized, knew of Louise and had, as many do, opinions about Louise and her work, but he did not know Marie and would not get to know her. That night, there would be a performance; the bearded poet would recite poems while playing a small transistor radio. He would sleep at an old friend's house, a friend he shared with Marie and who had worked with her to plan the performance. Marie was beginning to understand certain things about the bearded poet: he did not think much about wives, and felt himself generally above, which is to say, better than, domesticity and American dreams. She did not ask him, however, what he thought about lesbianism, even as she assumed that he, like so many well-meaning poets, would say he considered lesbians to be just the same as everybody else.

Marie could not remember why their mutual friend could not pick up the bearded poet from the airport, though she was increasingly grateful to not live in the same town as him, specifically or metaphorically, and over the years, she came to understand something more about their mutual friend's friendships with bearded men. The mutual friend, also a writer, loved the work of Violette Leduc, and like Leduc, she wrote stories about women struggling with feelings about other women, and unlike Leduc, the women in her stories did not have sex with each other or anyone else. In this way, the mutual friend also believed lesbians to be just like everyone else.

Several years later, Marie was measuring the walkway for a writing project when a woman pulled up in front of the house. "That fence is wrong," said Red, "and you know Parker didn't used to talk." Red's family had lived in the house for 52 years, including all of Red's childhood; she had driven by the house that morning because she was in the old neighborhood and wanted to see her childhood home. And there was Marie standing in the walkway, so she rolled down the passenger-side window and told Marie many things, like how hers was the first black family on the block and how the corner store sold liquor-laced candy to the children until Parker's mother found out; she almost put that store out of business, she was so mad. "None of us had fences," said Red, "because we wanted things open, and is that spirit still there in your upstairs hallway?" Marie shook her head, and Red scribbled down a phone number for Marie to call, saying, "Ask my sister, who used to see him—a bearded man, European, in an old-style, pinstripe suit."

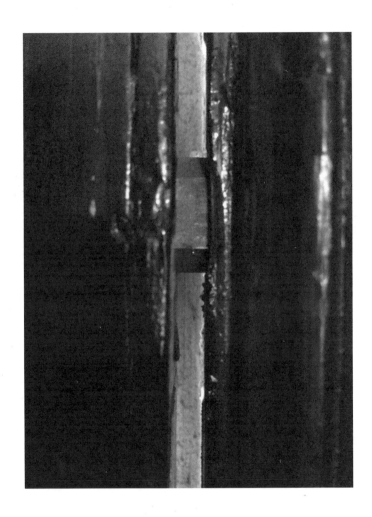

FRONT PARLOR

Women are supposed to be very calm, generally. Marie thought this a very strange sentence and wondered where it came from. "The more I write," she said, "the more I can't remember. I sometimes see an unnamed presence pressing between the words." Marie was speaking to the small group of women seated in the front parlor. Earlier that evening, Marianne Moore had helped Marie fill the parlor with chairs from the dining room and kitchen, and now all of the seats were taken and Marianne Moore was gathering information. "But tell me," said Marianne Moore, "what your sentence says about Mrs. Porter?" Marianne Moore was a poet with advanced degrees in literature and clinical psychology, and she was also the featured guest at that evening's art salon. In the past, the salon did not boast a special guest, or rather, each salon attendee had an equal amount of time to share anything she wanted, and anyone who came to the salon was required to share; but once the process became habitual it also became boring, and the women knew it was time for a change.

The women sat in front of a large pier-glass framed in walnut and flanked by two wooden columns. The pier-glass was built into the house, and as Marie glanced at it, she thought about Gwen Harwood, who once said she wanted a pier-glass just like that in her own bedroom. Gwen also said

Middlemarch was the most brilliant book of all time, though too bad the times have changed, so *Middlemarch* cannot be written again, or re-written, or written now. In *Middlemarch*, the pier-glass is a very important image, and in Marie's front parlor, the pier-glass reflected a Victorian mantel clock, gilded in gold and topped with a female figurine who held a pen in one hand and a piece of paper in the other. The clock was French and did not work. "The more I read, the more I write," said Marie, "and the more I write, the more I can't remember where or when something happened, in a dream or in a story. I can't remember," sighed Marie, "and I think Mrs. Porter is like that too." "But what are we trying to make?" asked Jean Rhys, who had become a frequent salon attendee. "And how," asked the recently tenured English professor, "does the salon's 'women-only' policy reflect Edmund Waller's lines: 'Tell me, lovely, loving pair! / Why so kind, and so severe? / Why so careless of our care, / Only to yourselves so dear?'"

The women called the salon "Mrs. Porter's" based on a character in T.S. Eliot's *The Waste Land*, and on other nights, at other Mrs. Porter's, women asked other questions, sometimes in their notebooks and sometimes sub-textually, and there were also very explicit questions, like the one about the whistling lesbians. "Are lesbians," asked a lesbian artist, "better whistlers than straight women?" The lesbian artist proceeded to lead the assembled women in a whistling song, and Marie, who could only whistle by sucking in and not blowing out, tried to whistle along with the others. Marie's poor whistling delighted Louise to no end, and Louise laughed and laughed and could not continue her whistling. This gave Marie such pleasure, she wished the two of them alone.

But that night, Marianne Moore was leading the women in a writing activity; she asked them to describe Mrs. Porter and to pretend the evening existed within Mrs. Porter's dream. "If I were to analyze Mrs. Porter's dream," said Marianne, "what would we learn about her make-up?"

"She would frown on poorly applied rouge," said Jean Rhys with a slight nod of her head, "and would know that being well-liked by many people would be good business sense," and with this, Jean Rhys tap-tapped her finger on the hard-cover book she held in her lap. "Mrs. Porter would definitely prefer HD to TS," said the recently-tenured English professor, who had been on an anti-Eliot tear for most the night. "Remember," said Julia Kristeva, "that Eliot's Mrs. Porter was based on a real person, a notorious brothel owner in Cairo during World War I." Julia Kristeva had been excavating Mrs. Porter from *The Waste Land* since the salon began ten years prior, and she had stories, too, about the Battle of Wozzer, or Wasa'a, or Wizzer—named after Cairo's red light district and the night soldiers rioted in protest of newly, or not-so-newly, contracted venereal disease. There were rumors, too, that the Battle of Wozzer broke out when an Australian soldier found his sister working in that notorious district, though the family thought she had been contracted as a domestic in a different country, likely European, and Mrs. Porter was, thought Marie, like so many women in life and literature—a surface for reflected desire. "Exactly," said Jean Rhys, "Mrs. Porter would know the power of rouge."

"I wonder," said Marianne Moore, as she leaned back and raised her eyebrows, "what that clock's figurine is writing." The women looked at the gold clock on the pier-glass mantel, and its female figure posed next to a desk, upon which lay a shining and open blank book.

Downstairs Bathroom

When Louise's mother died, she left a large gold-framed portrait of Louis XVIII and the women hung this picture over the bathroom sink in place of a mirror. This upset many dinner guests, who wanted, quite reasonably, to check their appearance in private. Yet most guests kept their upset to themselves, but the lesbian poet who wrote the novel told Louise it was cruel to not give guests this reflected image of themselves. Louise laughed, pointing to the many mirrors built into the house, and asked the lesbian poet if there was anything else she wanted to confess.

Louise and the lesbian poet continued to tease and argue, while Marie wondered at the ways writing teaches us to see ourselves and others. Earlier that day, she had written a story based on "The Female Cabin Boy," an early 18th century ballad about a woman who disguised herself as a male sailor, because that's what she needed to be in order to see the world. But out to sea, the ship's captain discovered her secret and immediately impregnated her, though not before the female cabin boy had a secret tryst with the captain's wife. Marie was writing a book about lesbians in literature, but she did not mention this to the lesbian poet because the lesbian poet wanted to talk to Louise only, and in this way, she was not unlike the bearded man.

Marie excused herself and went to the bathroom, which was small and painted a color called Union Blue; next to the toilet hung a small photograph of a President Garfield figurine and on the opposite wall hung a picture of a streetwalker in Rio de Janeiro. The pictures were taken by the same photographer—a woman Louise and Marie had published—and while the streetwalker wore female clothing, Marie did not assume the clothing determined genitalia, for gender is a costume, like the president, or a crown. Lesbianism is a costume too, thought Marie, as she glimpsed her own figure in Louis XVIII's glass covering. She would ask Louise for her thoughts later, after the lesbian poet left, for Louise, always so particular, insistent, and deeply thinking, would definitely have something long and big to say.

OFFICE

As a child, Marie believed what she was taught: that humans, especially Americans, were making progress in the world, becoming increasingly better and freer with each passing generation. Her teacher, for example, had attended Mass in Latin and was required to cover her head in church just because she was a girl. Young Marie was relieved the rules had changed; English-language Mass was easier and she liked keeping her head bare and free. The school uniform had also changed, so unlike her older sisters who wore plaid jumpers until they transferred to public high school, Marie wore pants to school, knowing she would also one day face decisions that her mother, or grandmother, didn't have or couldn't truly consider, like choosing birth control, or whether to just work a job or go for a career.

As a child, Marie was also taught that human society was becoming increasingly sinful. In the movies and on television, young people went to parties where they drank and had premarital sex, listening to lustful rock and roll music, and later, getting abortions as if they were ordering fast food hamburgers and fries, so innutritious, no wonder everyone walks around screaming and shooting at each other, adulterating and swearing, and everyone was getting divorced! These were the signs of modern times, and young Marie knew the situation was bad, even as she heard about other things getting better. Girls went to college now, and civil rights had happened; everyone was equal, she learned, and everyone had an equal chance. In college and through declined applications, Marie learned the myth of meritocracy. From sources outside college, she learned about homeowner enforced racial covenants, corporate redlining, and how the Federal Housing Administration insured loans in A-rated, generally white, neighborhoods but not in D-rated, mostly black, neighborhoods, creating a favorable climate in poor neighborhoods for loan sharks and other predatory lenders. Marie knew Parker grew up in the green house two doors down, and she thought about him buying the blue house with a VA loan— when did that happen?

The Washingtons bought their house in the late 1960s or early 70s after renting it for several years from a young white hippie who inherited the place from his grandmother. "This used to be a commune," said Mrs. Washington one afternoon, "and the whole outside was painted pink." Mrs. Washington did not think pink was a very good house color, and Marie mostly agreed, especially because it would have been rather unbelievable to describe a pink house on one side of them, and Parker's electric blue on the other. The Washingtons painted their house white, and like many people in the neighborhood, they did not fully scrape or sand before painting, so the paint bubbled and wore after just a few years. After all, thought Marie as she walked from Mrs. Washington's front porch to her own, it takes money to keep things picture-perfect, though when it comes down to it, who are we making the picture for? The white hippie had lived in San Francisco, and Mrs. Washington said he hadn't charged much for rent and also sold the house for real cheap. "He was a kind man," said Mrs. Washington. "He said he had enough money and didn't need to make more just because he could."

Marie had gone to the Washington's to give them a bag of lemons from the backyard tree, and to tell them that she and Louise would be away that weekend. They were leaving the teen children home alone for the first time, and Marie asked if she could give the children Mrs. Washington's number. Parker also agreed to keep an eye on the young people, and later, when Marie and Louise returned, they listened to Parker's late-night voicemail message asking the teens to please turn down the music. Yet the Washington's reported the teens' good behavior—Joelle Washington said she liked the sound of people having a good time—and Parker said the teens were no trouble, none at all. Everyone had, in fact, lived safely through the weekend, which was, thought Marie, a fact to remember, just like it's a fact that love is better than fear, and love often means repeatedly showing up and trying to see.

But there was a picture missing—a bawdy drawing of a mythical creature butt-fucking another mythical creature while a hermaphrodite grabbed their penis in one hand and their breast in the other. It was a small sketch in pencil by a Bay Area artist and it usually hung with a number of other pieces on the front staircase wall. It was a picture, as far as Marie knew, that the children barely noticed, though it reminded Marie of an early 18th century poem entitled "Monsieur Thing's Origin: or Seignior D---o's Adventures in Britain," about an Italian dildo that makes its way to London and has quite the time. One doesn't expect to read a dildo poem written anonymously in 1722; then again, the more Marie learned, the more she realized how much was buried. The children swore they knew nothing about the picture, and to Marie's relief, it appeared a few days later in Louise's office, tucked behind another frame and turned so the bawdy scene faced the wall.

BEDROOM 2

Inside the tall, narrow cupboard sat several unused bottles of tempera paint. The cupboard was built into the smallest bedroom, and the paint had belonged to the Whittle's son, a tall skinny boy who was one year older than Marie and Louise's daughter. Their daughter, who shall now be called Colette after that great French writer, immediately claimed the smallest room for herself, and as she liked to paint and draw, she eventually created large murals on all four walls. Behind her door, she drew the top part of a sturdy tree, pasting cutouts of small creatures on the penciled branches. "Did you know," said Marie to her daughter, "the basement walls used to be covered with murals. They were painted by Red's father, the LAPD officer, who also hosted dances in the basement and played the violin." Colette paused and raised her eyebrows wide. "Do you think this house is haunted?" she asked.

Unlike their daughter, the French writer Colette was married three times, and her first husband, Willy, locked her in a room and made her write books that he published under his name, not hers. After Colette left him, she supported herself, in part, as a vaudeville dancer and mime. She also had a six-year relationship with Mathilde de Morny, more commonly known as Missy, and from various accounts and rumors, it seemed the two women delighted in a bit of public scandal and dramatic effect. Meanwhile, Colette continued to write, eventually publishing *Gigi* and *Chéri and Le Pur et l'impur*, which was translated into English as *The Pure and the Impure*. A novel comprised of sexual portraits, *The Pure and the Impure* was based on people Colette knew, and when she wrote, she did not change their names. It was, she said, the closest thing to an autobiography she had written. It was not, however, a book highly favored by critics; a reviewer for the *New York Times* said it "lacks excuse for being," and while we know a book is not exactly the same as a living breathing human, such a comment raises questions about the purpose of books in general. Does a book need a reason to be, and if a book repeatedly included the phrase—*please, excuse me for being*—would that make the book more acceptable to more people? What kind of people feel the need to excuse their being, and when Virginia Woolf's uncle, Sir James Fitzjames Stephen, wrote that a novel should be "a biography," did he believe that any life, of any person, would do? These are, Marie knew, age-old poetic questions, yet they were questions Marie and Louise considered quite frequently, for as writers and publishers, they made books in a variety of ways. About her own poetry, Louise maintained one should never apologize, never explain.

Having children is not the same as having a book, for even though a book can have a life of its own, it does not necessarily experience the consciousness of feeling itself read. Childishness, however, can trouble any number of adults, including those who are parents. In *The Pure and the Impure*, Colette included a portrait of Renée Vivian, calling her initially by her birth name, Pauline Tarn, and describing her youthful face as roguish with a "propensity to laughter." According to Colette, Vivian never ceased to claim an affinity with Lesbos, and Marie sensed that Colette considered such a life-time affinity as somewhat immature. After all, Colette dated women but married men, and one of the women Colette dated was Natalie Barney who had been, more significantly, Renée Vivian's great love. Barney wrote that Colette got Vivian all wrong; Vivian died young and Barney later described Vivian's life as a long suicide, while Colette wondered if Vivian's abyss was real or imagined. "Ghouls," wrote Colette, "are rare."

"Do you remember," said Colette to Marie, "when I was little and asked if ghosts were real and you said, 'Maybe'?" Marie bit her lip guiltily as Colette laughed, "You really freaked me out!"

FRONT UPSTAIRS PORCH

Marie often thought about the good Anna who came to the United States from Germany and who scolded her dogs for their naughty behavior. Marie also scolded her dogs for doing things dogs tend to do, like eating food or condoms found on the streets and sniffing human crotches. Stein wrote: "The good Anna had high ideals for canine chastity and discipline." Unlike the good Anna, Marie did not care about chastity—human or canine—though she did stop her dogs from creating more puppies and she also insisted on canine obedience and cuddles. She called her dogs Miss Furr and Miss Skeene, and she liked to lie on the floor with the two of them, one dog on either side, and pet them as she said: "We are regularly gay, aren't we ladies? We are gay, so must do gay things everyday, they don't see us, so they say, we are gay and only gay," and with that, Marie rubbed Miss Furr's belly with one hand as she scratched Miss Skeene's head with the other.

There was a lovely breeze on the front upstairs porch, but that evening, Marie was focused on the pigeons. They had made a nest on one of its bungalow-style columns, and pigeon feathers and guano piled up on the porch floor and railing, falling unto the front steps below and smearing the front of the house, and this was not good. Marie used a broom to brush at the pigeons, and while one of the pigeons flew away, two pigeons stayed in the nest. Marie looped Louise into her pigeon project, asking Louise to please stand on the porch and catch the hose as Marie tossed it in the air, and Louise, who Marie considered to be an especially fine catch, caught the hose and held it as she waited for Marie. Back upstairs and on the front porch, Marie sprayed water at the guano and feathers, and she sprayed near the two sitting pigeons, and still the pigeons stayed. "Oh dear," said Marie, as she walked back into Louise's office, closing the front porch door behind her. "Those are teen pigeons and they cannot fly!"

Marie thought about Gertrude Stein's sentences much more than she thought about Stein's lines. "Stein's sentences," she said, "move along like shifting consciousness, so you have the repetition of daily living, and the words, which are both semiotic units and representations, slowly shifting in their meaning via their relationship to each other, like how we come to have relationships with other people, and with words and things." Marie laughed then, and felt embarrassed and long-winded and overly academic. She was speaking to the two interns who were in the office that day, the day after she sprayed near the pigeons, and she had already repeated the teen pigeon story to the interns, who said "Oh no!" and who agreed that adolescence is a tricky and dangerous time. "I had to move the teen pigeons," Marie had said, "though they were perfectly happy to sit and do nothing." The interns, who were happy to no longer be teens themselves, sighed with Marie over the sad story of the pigeons, for Marie had placed the birds in a box and put the box on a picnic table in the back yard, and that night, another creature—most likely a pussy and not a pup—came and slowly circled the box, moving in, closer and closer; in the morning, there were only pigeon feathers lying around.

BACK FOYER

The back foyer was the warmest room in the house. Its glass-paned French doors were not covered by curtains or blinds, so the sun streamed into the room unresisted, fading the cork floor and heating the space. Besides the door mat, the only object in the room was a chrome trash can with a broken foot pedal, which meant everyone living in or visiting the house had to manually lift the can's lid to throw their trash away. Marie had moved the trash can to the back foyer because Miss Furr, the small dog, could also lift the lid in order to pull bits of trash and eat them. Marie worried that Miss Furr's indiscriminate eating would one day do the small dog in, and she worried that writing such a worry would help the worry manifest as true. She also worried about the amount of trash they produced, the shifting climate and the ever-growing trash islands in more than one ocean, though she knew that she and Louise would never do as two of their friends had done: save all their trash for a year or two, especially the plastic, and turn it into art.

But, thought Marie, I am trying to be very honest. It's true: I was sitting on the back foyer floor the first time I read work by Helen Rose Hull. The dogs were outside; I waited for them and felt forlorn and melancholy as I wondered why I didn't already know about Hull and her lifelong partner, Mabel Louise Robinson. Marie was reading one of Hull's

Cynthia stories, about a young woman who came of age in the American midwest; as she read, Marie thought again about how books starring adolescent boys are frequently held up as representative of a generation, while books starring girls are never thought to represent boys. Cynthia did not want to hurt her mother, nor did she want to live a life enclosed by useful, homely things: is this not a conflict felt by many? Perhaps, thought Marie, Helen Rose Hull's writing is simply not as good as Ernest Hemingway's or J.D. Salinger's; then again, when she looked up Helen Rose Hull in the American National Biography (ANB) Online—its byline reads *The life of a nation is told by the lives of its people*—Helen Rose Hull was not included, despite her 17 books, national reputation, and awards like the Guggenheim Fellowship, but Marie saw the ANB did include an entry for Andy Adams, who wrote *The Log of a Cowboy: A Narrative of the Old Trail Days*, and Marie remembered how Virginia Woolf was considered a minor writer until relatively recently, and so we return to the question of who is reading whom.

Marie's friend, Leonora Carrington, hated words like "minor" or "major" to describe various writers and writing; she considered a book to be a consciousness that grew and shifted over time, because everyone's reading and writing around a book makes the book too. Leonora Carrington thought a lot about the kinds of consciousness she wrote into the world; in one story, Leonora wrote: "The painting that Rose re-paints everyday is semi-mimetic, full of shapes that could be trees or humans or animals or houses or areas of commerce; or, it could be semi-abstract, just color and harmonic alone, with semi-recognizable symbols." Reading, thought Marie, makes the painting more or less abstract or mimetic, and critical consensus comes when some people convince other people to see the way they read.

Which returns us to legibility, said Marie, aloud and to herself. She had, by this time, moved to the more familiar green chair in the second parlor where she made the following notes about writing: 1) do you need to be listed in history as proof of your existence; 2) how can you avoid leaving a trash-filled consciousness in the world; 3) while many writers will chase attention, money, or status, how will you remember the words of Leonora Carrington: "I have decided not to be hungry."

Upstairs Bathroom 1

Spangled Unicorn is the title of a fake anthology of modernist verse first published in London in 1932. More accurately, *Spangled Unicorn* is a fictional, satirical anthology of modernist verse written by Noël Coward, who was much better known as a composer and playwright, but who, for this particular book, wrote a number of fictional biographies of fictional poets complete with their fictional-yet-very-real verse. Each fictional poet was based on a real poet Coward knew, which makes for a fun matching game. Coward included, for example, the imaginary Jane Southerby Danks, his portrayal of Radclyffe Hall, infamous author of the infamous lesbian novel *The Well of Loneliness*. The imaginary Danks wrote from a whaling ship off the coast of Helsinforth and she was quite repulsed by the Sous Realist School of writers. She wrote boating songs and ballads, to wit: "They brew good beer at the 'Saucy Sheep' / With a derry dun derry and soon may be."

Marie quite enjoyed the *Spangled Unicorn* poems and sank happily into the idea of Coward's anthology. She would, she thought, like to edit/write *Spangled Unicorn 2*, an obvious blockbuster sequel. She would ask her friend James Tiptree, Jr. to come on as co-editor, and together they would imagine any number of mostly queer writers as fictionalized versions of themselves. The book would include a smattering of straight poets, including the queer-curious and/or queer-affected, plus a number of self-identified queers who had since married or partnered up with people of the opposite sex and/or gender. Marie would insist, however, that they adamantly reject all poems in which the speaking "I" is a hyper-straight female who wears silver-pink glitter and writes about being ass-fucked by a stupid silly sexy man, not unlike the kind of man who gets off by listening to her poem. "Ixnay on the princess-tableau fantasies too," Marie would say to James Tiptree, Jr., though she would later reverse this position when James Tiptree, Jr. showed her the bio and poem he wrote portraying the fictional Lucie Leonardo-Clay, an up-and-coming poet who made big waves in her adopted coastal city. Lucie compensated for her family's wealth and inherited sense of self-worth by publically acknowledging her privilege through a series of online videos, in which she appeared, skinny and toned and almost always nearly naked as she said, "I am rich and want to be broken." A mild controversy surrounded Lucie Leonardo-Clay, with some poets calling her courageous and an honest show of surface, while others critiqued her boob show (too sexy/not sexy enough), and still others shrugged and turned toward what they called better, near-perfect things.

Meanwhile, James Tiptree, Jr. would insist that at least one of the poets be from a local chapter of the Red Hat Society, and that perhaps they should travel to the Society's next International Convention to scope the talent. Marie would happily agree, for the Society grew from a Jenny Joseph poem, which was also the title of an anthology published in 1991, and Marie had that book when she was first discovering feminism, and Marie needed feminism before she could find writing. Marie then suggested including at least one member of a straight male activist group dedicated to fighting the popular image of poetry as a sissy art by giving readings in a wide-legged stance. Such men annoyed James Tiptree, Jr., who subsequently made a very cogent argument for the inclusion of at least one, if not two or more, super poignant straight-girl-being-fucked-while-wearing-glitter poems, and he told Marie that perhaps she needed to check her judgments for there are many ways to use glitter while telling *that* guy to fuck off into the sea.

Marie imagined this while preparing, then soaking in the large claw-foot tub installed in the main bathroom, a tub older than, and as purposeful as, Coward's anthology. She had added full-moon salts to her bath, and as she cupped her hands and splashed the salty moon water on her face, she realized—with the dreamiest lucidity ever—that the line stuck in her head for the past several days would make the perfect *Spangled Unicorn 2* epigraph:

"What do ye do when ye see a whale, men?"

Upstairs Bathroom 2

One afternoon, after vacuuming and before showering, Marie left the small bathroom to lie on the bed in the adjacent bedroom and think about Mary Renault. Marie was undressed, but she was not having sexy thoughts. Instead, she wondered about Renault growing older alongside her sweetheart, Julie Mullard, and how the two women had moved to South Africa after Renault won a writing prize that came with a big cash award. They picked South Africa because, as rumors or interviews report it, they found it less repressive than their native Britain; this was in the 1950s and Mary and Julie were white.

Before becoming a full-time writer, Mary Renault worked as a nurse, as did Julie Mullar; it seemed the two women met on the job. Marie's good friend, Phoebe Gloeckner, was also dating a nurse, though because Phoebe was a professor, a writer, and a lesbian—not in that order—she did not meet her nurse at work. When Marie told Phoebe Gloeckner that she was writing a lesbianic book, Phoebe laughed and said, "Aren't they all?" Marie understood this as Phoebe's way of saying that being gay is to write gayness; then again, Phoebe could be referring to the primacy of desire as integral to the creative act. Unlike Marie, Phoebe Gloeckner frequently wrote about her own lesbian experiences, so perhaps Phoebe was speaking and projecting her own process onto writers and writing in general as part of her ongoing negotiation between the borders of herself and others. Phoebe, like Marie, was deeply interested in intersubjectivity, and in general, she very much liked and needed to process her feelings and relationships, and Marie considered Phoebe's processing as one of her charming, lesbianic qualities.

Over the years, Marie watched Phoebe struggle with being in- and excluded from a group of lesbian writers who toured around the country performing lesbian identities. This often meant sharing their real life sexy thoughts and exploits, which made them generally more popular than lesbian writers who did not, for varying artistic and/or philosophical reasons, write from a knowable, tangible, seemingly transparent lesbian "I." "But I want to be popular," Phoebe repeatedly told Marie, "and I *know* it won't make me happy!"

By the time Mary Renault died, she was known for writing historical novels about homosexual male relationships in ancient Greece, and these books, more popular than her lesbianic- or nurse-themed work, were not valued for their historical accuracy but for their spot-on reflections of a contemporary psychological moment. Spot-on, thought Marie as she rose from bed still naked and quickly walked toward the shower.

BEDROOM 3

When Marie and Louise went out of town, they liked to ask someone to stay over and take care of Miss Furr and Miss Skeene. The caretakers were often interns, or former interns, who already knew the dogs, having worked in the basement with Marie. Most of the interns were young writers, and Marie wondered what they thought as they stayed in the bedroom, sleeping and also likely reading. Sometimes, after she and Louise returned home, Marie caught glimpses into the people who had stayed—if the time had been pleasant or burdensome or almost too upsetting and whether she could or would ask them again.

Years before, Marie had worked cleaning other couples' houses and sometimes these couples divorced, informing Marie of the change in a note left on the kitchen counter and usually stating they no longer needed her service. Marie cleaned houses for two years, and during that time, three couples divorced; Marie always knew there was a problem before the actual separation, so the note never came as a surprise. When people are having troubles, they leave little or big signs, like the wife who left her vibrator in the young daughter's room where she had been sleeping, or the lesbian couple who began separating their laundry, which was a marked shift from how they'd been before. At the time, Marie was also in graduate school, learning about writing, and one of the couples she cleaned for—two young attorneys with an old house and a regularly pleasant sex life—were excited about Marie's possibilities as a writer and hoped she would write about them. For the holiday, they gave her a book they'd heard about on NPR—a memoir written by a lesbian who cleaned other people's houses, saying perhaps Marie would someday turn her job into stories. Later, when the male attorney asked Marie how she liked the book, she nodded and said it was funny; she said this in politeness, for the book was fine—the meal equivalent of seasalt pita chips dipped in garlic hummus—but Marie would never read the book again, secretly thinking it was not the kind of book she wanted to write.

Later, when Marie was no longer a housecleaner but a publisher, it seemed everyone she spoke to already knew about William Carlos Williams and his red wheelbarrow. So much depended on them knowing this small poem and their opinion of the poem indicated something about their view of poetry. When Marie was a housecleaner, she listened to many books and lectures on tape, including a book by a writer who practiced Zen meditation and wrote self-help books for writers. You learn to write by writing, said the writer with her nasal, New York accent, and then she read "The Red Wheelbarrow," saying the poem was a poem because Williams saw a red wheelbarrow after the rain, and either the moment awoke, or he awoke in that moment.

But did Williams see or know Maura and Ethel, the principle characters of his story entitled "The Knife of the Times"? Marie considered this question, while wondering what makes a story different than a poem. Maura and Ethel were childhood friends, and after they married, Maura moved to New York City and Ethel moved to Harrisburg, where she wrote letters to Maura, who, in the beginning, always showed them to her husband. But over time, Ethel's letters became increasingly passionate, not unlike what a man might send to a woman, and the letters confused Maura, who hid them away and no longer mentioned Ethel at dinner or during cab rides. The story ends right before the two women become lovers, and Ethel is fully awake to the situation, while Maura goes along with Ethel's desires because, as Maura says, "Why not?" Marie wondered about "the times" of the story and also who, or what, was the knife, for the story's only knife is in its title, which makes it more symbolic than mimetic. Is that how the two women-lesbian-characters were too?

Over the years, Marie had held a wide variety of jobs. In addition to housecleaner, she had been a telemarketer, a WIC certifier, a waitress, a grant writer, a writing tutor, a middle school teacher, factory packager, dishwasher, retail salesperson, snack bar cashier, adjunct professor, event coordinator, publisher, and more. Over the years, many people told her such a background was good for a writer, though as Marie grew older and increasingly knew even more published writers, she was often surprised at how few of them had ever worked in service jobs or for minimum wage. She knew of one rather politically-minded writer who consistently failed to recognize his work-study students at their jobs in the school cafeteria, likely because the students wore cafeteria aprons and hair nets not unlike the other, non-student workers, and apparently their professor, the writer, did not distinguish one worker from the next. Marie was also surprised to learn of various poets' rich relations, like the self-identified Marxist whose parents owned a multi-million dollar compound in Malibu, where he and other Marxist poets stayed when visiting the city. She had learned, too, about various well-published cousins, aunts and uncles who held positions in powerful places, and the networks of poets and writers who first met when they were together at Brown or Yale or Iowa, or who had studied under the same relatively famous poet, vowing to keep that poet's memory alive. But there were skills to learn too, alongside the gossip, like how to supervise interns as someone who was also unpaid;

the interns came from a wide variety of backgrounds, and in Marie's opinion, experience in service work was a definite plus. How does a person's daily routine—at the job and in the bedroom—influence her imagination; Marie pondered this as she later pulled weeds in the back yard garden, and she heard Parker call his dog a dirtbag and wondered what the poor creature had done.

Meanwhile, in the house, Marie and Louise's bedroom was almost 100% completely furnished with items inherited from Louise's mother, and this made the bedroom feel less personal but more luxurious than other bedrooms Marie had known.

KITCHEN

"But I haven't read that either," said Marie, as she closed the oven door and set the chrome time inexactly for 12-13 minutes.

"But you've probably read more than you realize," said Franz Kafka. He sat at the square, stone-top kitchen table, watching Marie and drinking black coffee, despite the late afternoon hour. Drinking coffee did not keep Franz Kafka awake when he wanted to sleep, and this was one of the many small things he and Marie had in common. Marie poured herself a cup of coffee and sat down opposite Franz. "It's true," said Franz Kafka, "think about it." "It's true for you," said Marie, for rarely did she mention a book that Franz had not already read. "Good stuff," Franz would say if he liked or admired a book. Franz Kafka often spoke in short, one- to three-word summations, and he tended to write short sentences and sentence fragments as well, though not all of his sentences were short. "Many, but not all," Franz would say, and when Marie thought of Franz Kafka's writing, she very rarely saw quotation marks, for while Franz wrote fiction, his prose did not move between scene and summary in a conventionally realistic way. He did not write many descriptions of food; he rarely described people eating.

"You don't write about food very much, do you?" said Marie. "People have to eat," said Franz Kafka, and the timer rang so Marie stood up to check the cookies. They were vegan cookies made with oatmeal, whole wheat flour, canola oil, cinnamon, nutmeg, baking soda, vanilla, brown sugar, soy milk, sea salt, water, and sometimes ground ginger, orange juice and/or zest, and clove. They were Louise's favorite kind of cookie, and Franz Kafka, who was relaxed but particular about what he ate, also liked to eat them. "I don't write about food very much either," said Marie, "but Louise does." "I know," said Franz Kafka.

The kitchen was pleasant; Whittles had renovated it, installing cream-colored cupboards, sandstone counters, cork floor, and a six range Dutch oven, which was much fancier than anything Marie and Louise would have purchased. "Tell me again," said Marie, "what you dislike about close third." "I don't dislike close third," said Franz Kafka, who had, perhaps, grown accustomed to being slightly misunderstood. "But people, other writers, have called my work 'close third,' as if I was really using a 'fake first.' It's lazy reading, like the 'he' in the writing was me, not even the narrator, but me, Franz, the writer."

"And you are a real character, you know," said Marie with a teasing smile, and Franz Kafka laughed.

"That is a sentence."

"I've been reading Marcia Davenport's *Of Lena Geyer*— a novel written as a fake biography of an early 20th century opera singer. The narrator is a young music enthusiast, and he includes long, multi-page passages of other people's encounters with Lena Geyer, especially their meals, and everything gets very swirly, who is speaking, eating, or seeing who."

"I like playing with perspective, forgetting the 'I,' trying something new, like mimicking Louise or Marcia Davenport, and writing something, more or less, about food."

Front Stairway

Denis Sanguin de Saint-Pavin's love poem, "Two Beauties, Tender Lovers," published in 1650, portrays two women so equally distressed, neither of them can orgasm despite their switching up of sex roles, wooing hard to get the other off: "Now the one lover is mistress / Now the mistress is lover." Yet Saint-Pavin appears satisfied with such poetic justice; after all, these are the same two women who, as he wrote earlier, "refuse their pleasures to us."

This "us" addressed to the reader vexed Marie. Everyone is writing to some imaginary audience, even if she says she never thinks about the reader; as soon as a writer imagines where his work might be published, the audience already inside him begins to emerge. Audience, thought Marie, connects to content and pronouns, and from where she stood in the foyer, she looked up at the front staircase and imagined an unknown figure's slow descent. She would see their legs first, the side of their body, their head would be hidden by a wall until they reached the tenth or eleventh stair down, then only four more steps before two turns to the left, and here the figure is: standing in front of Marie.

It had been a long, not bad, but full day, with much writing and also a visit from Donald Barthelme, a former intern. Donald Barthelme was proof that lesbians do not need men for child-raising or orgasms, as Donald's mothers had been together for nearly 35 years, and in that time, Marie assumed and hoped, they shared sexual satisfaction. Marie planned on being with Louise for at least that long and even longer, though neither she nor Louise were the sort who kissed and told.

Most people do not want to imagine their moms having sex. When Marie hired Donald Barthelme, she correctly guessed that he was gay, but did not know he was the child of lesbians, just as he likely guessed that Marie a lesbian, though he didn't know The Press was run by lesbian mothers. What happy synchronicities!

Donald Barthelme interned for two consecutive summers, and one evening during the second summer, he and Marie spoke together at an after-event party Marie and Louise were hosting at their house. There had been some strange activity in the house lately; in addition to the mysteriously moved bawdy drawing, someone, or something, was drinking apple juice stored in the pantry, and not bothering to refrigerate the bottles once they were opened, though again, the children swore it was not them. Donald Barthleme told Marie about the several times he had seen ghosts, and the stories chilled Marie for they were strange and Donald was a level-headed reasonable guy. Marie told Donald some of her ghost stories from previous apartments: the light that kept coming on, the bald figure who walked through the living room, the small child in knickers, the cold spot by her parents' back door. "But," said Marie, "I haven't necessarily felt a continuous presence here," and Donald Barthelme said he hadn't either, but as he would be dog sitting later that month, he agreed to keep his ears and eyes primed.

.

FRONT PORCH STEPS

Miss Skeene tripped as she ran down the front porch steps, tumbling past the rosemary bushes and face-planting on the cement walkway, skinning her muzzle and foreleg. Yet she was back up within moments, barking at the young man on the sidewalk who pushed a toddler in a stroller shaped like a pink car, complete with steering wheel and seat belt. Marie ran out behind the dog, laughing at her clumsiness and scolding her to please quiet down.

The stroller was dirty and the toddler began to cry. Marie heard her name as Miss Skeene turned and began barking at Parker, who stood against the side fence, his face peeking through a large tangle of overgrown vines. "Are you going to trim these soon?" he said, extending his arm to Miss Skeene. The dog took some quick sniffs and continued to bark as Marie looked at the mess of vines and thought about her many obligations. She had just been reading Marina Tsvetaeva's line—"loves for love's sake is childhood"—which reminded her of Colette calling Renée Vivian childish and Saint-Pavin's depiction of girlish lesbians who refused to oblige the men.

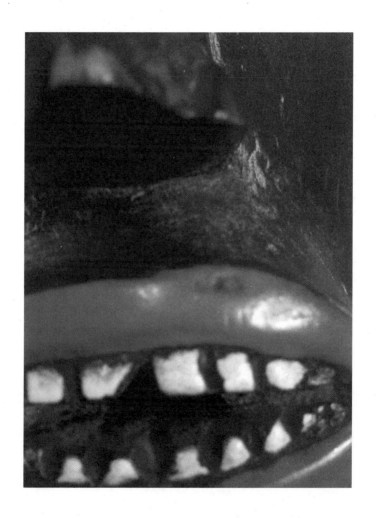

UPSTAIRS HALLWAY

To make space for a painting, the women decided to move two bookcases into the upstairs hallway. Louise, like the children, was initially against this plan, but Marie convinced them it was the only option. Louise relented, though on the condition of a general book cull. There were an extraordinary number of books in the house, and Louise liked to go through them at least once a year to make space for new reading.

The annual book cull went like this:

Louise began with a random shelf. She moved quickly, pulling out books in a split second decision.

Marie followed behind, picking up each title Louise had pulled out and wondering if she would like to read it, that day or in the future.

Marie asked Louise if the book was good.

Louise said it was fine or okay or alright, but she would never read it again.

Sometimes Louise shrieked and said no. She bought it because she had to. She knew the person. In some cases, Marie knew, or had known, the person as well.

Marie pointed out that the book was personally inscribed to Louise.

Louise said something about the person who wrote the inscription.

The person who wrote the inscription was often a former teacher, classmate, or acquaintance, who over the years, quit approving of Louise and Marie and the books they published. Sometimes, less rarely, Louise did not know the person, or the person was long dead.

Sometimes, as Marie was putting a book back on the shelf, she noticed another book she'd never read.

This was how she discovered Ronald Firbank's *The Flower Beneath the Foot*, published in 1924.

The epigraph was ascribed to St. Laura de Nazianzi: "Some girls are born organically good: I wasn't."

Eventually, everyone grew accustomed to the hallway's new look.

BACK DECK STEPS

Marie snapped a photo of the gay male writers seated on the two-person rocker at the top of the back deck steps. The photo would, she knew, be a hit on the internet, and because it was a new season—at The Press and in the lives of the women—and the garden party had been re-imagined as a Summer Solstice event.

"Our sun," said Phoebe Gloeckner as she instructed guests to drop flower petals around a small fire, "is a freak. For this Solstice ritual," she continued, "I wanted to acknowledge the bizarre atypical aspects of the solar system, and its central star, our sun; may we express our intentions or vows to notice, accept, appreciate, and encourage aspects of oddity in ourselves and other beings, for the benefit of all and according to free will."

"At the Stein-Toklas parties," wrote Janet Flanner in an essay published after Alice B. Toklas's death, "the gentlemen would congregate loyally around Gertrude, while we ladies would be grouped around the tea table presided over by Alice, so we could get the gossip." Flanner described Toklas's efforts to ensure Stein's "literary immortality" by printing her unpublished manuscripts. Stein's estate provided money for printing and for Alice to live on, but the court-appointed administrator of the estate—named Edgar Allen Poe, and he was, in fact, the poet's great nephew—often made Alice's life more difficult with his disapproving ways.

Louise observed, matter-of-factly, that this was not her party; she was spreading frosting over Marie's broken bundt cake (lemon-flavored, and it did not want to come out of its pan), and they served the cake alongside dozens of vegan cupcakes plus ice-cream made by Judith Butler, the new board member.

"I'm adopting a homopseudonym," Marie later told Louise, after the guests had gone and Marie had finished reading a new book by one of the women who performed at the party; the woman was married to one of the photographed gay men and she wrote about making meaning and being present in one's life, ending the book with: "I will never die."

DINING ROOM

Louise and Marie had a dinner party. All the guests were lesbians, a happy coincidence more than plan. Mina Loy was visiting from the small town of lesbians and loggers, and Phoebe Gloeckner was also free that night. Esther McCoy and Claire Denis arrived carrying beer and rosé wine; as they entered, they kissed Vija Celmins on both cheeks. Vija Celmins brought two salads—tomato and chicken papaya—and as most of the women were no longer eating wheat, Louise provided steak and foie gras.

The women sat at the dining room table, and Marie worried again about the uncomfortably hard chairs. It had been especially hot that summer, and as Marie opened one of the bay windows, she saw Alisa in the next door window; the two women waved hello. An unusually large close-up photograph of the back of a woman's head was propped up against one of the dining room windows. The woman wore a red sweater embroidered with small, four-petal flowers, though the flower in between her shoulder blades was missing its top two petals, leaving what looked like a tiny pair of useless wings. Behind the woman, in the blurry distance, sat a man in a suit; the woman, it seemed, was being interviewed, and the man was likely one man in a long line of similarly-suited men. The woman's dark hair was combed in a bob, and Marie could see floating single strands.

"Today," said Marie, "is Herman Melville's birthday."

Louise asked if anyone had read *Pierre*. Several women shook their heads, and Louise laughed as she described the book—a gothic, domestic land drama full of incest, though if she remembered correctly, he was trying to write something that would appeal to a larger reading public, especially the ladies, but you don't always, if ever, get to pick the kind of writing you'll make.

"And the incest was about the writing too," said Marie. "Pierre is writing a book, and perhaps the book he writes is the book we are reading, though its not self-referential in this way... oh, and incest in gothic novels is often about controlling blood lines, which is, I suppose true for Pierre, in a very convoluted way, so even the incest isn't pure."

"Impure incest is pretty good," said Mina Loy, "but do you know about Katherine Harris Bradley and Edith Emma Cooper?"

Again, the women shook their heads.

"They wrote under the penname Michael Field, and all of these male artists and writers, like Browning, Wilde, Meredith and Ruskin, liked their work and gave it a big critical stamp of approval, until they discovered that 'Michael Field' was actually two women—two lesbians who were also lovers—and that bunched the men up in panty-knots, so they had to backtrack and say Michael Field's work wasn't so good after all. But the best part"—Mina Loy paused, tapping her fingers together, palm-side in—"was that Katherine Harris Bradley was Edith Emma Cooper's aunt."

"Oh, that's good!" exclaimed Louise.

"Edith's mom, who was Katherine's sister, died when Edith was a baby, so Aunt Katherine moved in to help raise the child. She was 18 years older than Edith, and when Edith became a teenager, they started sleeping together, or rather, family love got sexy. The women lived together for the rest of their lives and died just three days apart, both from cancer."

Esther McCoy and Phoebe Gloeckner laughed as Louise's eyes glittered, for it was a good story of grooming, incest, and the kind of true-lovers' shared death that comes when a book ends.

Louise said one time she had a palm reading by the experimental prose writer who was also Clarice Lispector's psychic teacher; she told Louise that Marie should write a book about publishing.

"A how-to book!" said Phoebe. "I can illustrate it."

"But Marie," said Claire Denis, who had been intently watching and listening and who now looked at Marie very directly.

"Tell me, what do you write?"